Hawk

T

Tony Reno

High Noon Books
Novato, California

Editor: Jim Arena
Cover Art: Jim McConnell
Cover Design: Bonnie Gatter
Illustrations: Jim McConnell

International Standard Book Number: 1-57128-330-7

14 13 12 11 10 09 08 07 06 05
10 09 08 07 06 05 04 03 02 01

Contents

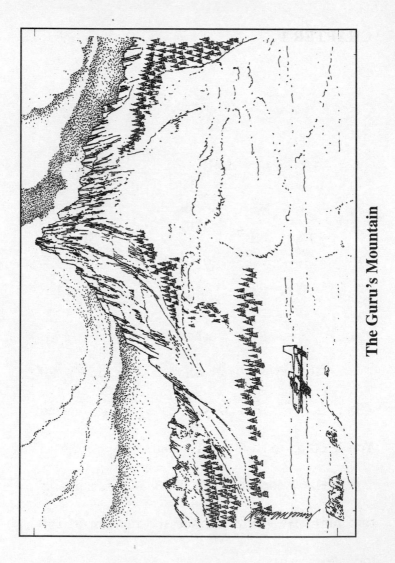

The Guru's Mountain

CHAPTER 1

The Hour of the Wolf

Hawk Davidson was standing on the top of a tall mountain. It was very bright, but Hawk felt cold. A shadowy figure stood next to him.

"Who are you?" asked Hawk.

"It doesn't matter who I am, Hawk. It's not about me. It's not about your gear. It's about you. You're going to have to trust yourself."

Hawk looked down. He was thousands of feet high. He could not see the bottom of the mountain.

"Trust yourself, Hawk," the figure said.

Hawk released himself from his harness.

He fell 10 feet, 20 feet, 30 feet, 50 feet, 100 feet...

Hawk woke to the sound of his cell phone. He rolled over in his bed and looked at the clock. It was 3:24 a.m. Ever since Hawk had been working for ACME Extreme Sports, he never turned his cell phone off. He reached over in the dark and flipped open the phone.

"Hello," said Hawk.

"Hawk, is that you?"

"Yeah....what is it?" Hawk replied as he was trying to wake up.

2

"This is Mick. I'm at the ACME building. You need to come here now."

"Uh...ACME...," Hawk was still waking up.

"Hawk, pay attention," Mick said, "the Bosses want to talk to you."

"Yeah, OK...ACME...Bosses..." Hawk muttered.

"Hawk, listen. The Bosses are expecting you in 30 minutes. Be there."

"All right, all right, I'll be there," Hawk said as he ended the call.

CHAPTER 2

Meeting with the Bosses

Hawk Davidson was very good at a lot of different sports. In fact, he was one of the top extreme athletes world-wide. Hawk also worked for ACME Extreme Sports. He tested sports gear for them.

The ACME building was only a few miles from Hawk's house. He drove his motor cycle into the parking lot. It was 3:54 a.m.

Hawk went into the ACME boardroom. The room was large and dark. In it was a huge long table and a giant TV screen on the wall. The Bosses sat on the left and right sides of the table.

Hawk could see Mick sitting with them. Mick was ACME's mechanic. Mick also flew helicopters and planes for ACME. He was also a good friend. Hawk wondered why he was sitting with the Bosses.

"Sit down, Hawk," said Boss 4. "I'd like to thank you for coming at such an odd hour."

"No problem, just as long as you are paying me double," Hawk snapped.

"We have a good reason for getting you here, Hawk," said Boss 2.

"Maybe someone is going to tell me what it is," Hawk replied.

5

"For years we have heard about a person living at the top of a mountain in Antarctica," Boss 2 said. "He is a master athlete. In fact, he's so good that people call him the Guru. We think that RIVAL is trying to find him."

"What's that got to do with me?" Hawk asked.

Boss 5 then spoke, "We think the Guru has invented something, possibly a new snowboard. We think that RIVAL wants to steal the snowboard and make copies so they can sell it."

"How do you know this?" Hawk asked.

"RIVAL may be bigger than us, but we have our own spies," Boss 6 said.

"If RIVAL gets this snowboard, every

snowboarder will want one. It could ruin us, Hawk," Boss 4 added.

"We want to get our hands on it first," said Boss 5.

"Why me?" Hawk asked.

"You have had a lot of experience with RIVAL. And you can think fast. You may need all your skills for this one," said Boss 7.

"And what if I find this Guru before RIVAL?" Hawk asked.

"You mean *we* find the Guru," Mick finally spoke. "I'm going with you, Hawk."

"Well, that makes me feel better – I think," Hawk said.

CHAPTER 3

Getting There

It was the next day about 11:00 a.m. Hawk and Mick had already made one stop in South America. Now they were flying in an ACME C-130 Hercules plane. It was made to land on flat ice fields. Hawk checked his pack: two ACME ice-axes, a pair of boots with ice crampons, wool pants and gloves, a climbing harness, ropes, screws, a thermos of water, five Power Bars, and an ACME snowboard.

"Got everything?" Mick asked.

"I hope so," Hawk answered. "We are halfway into Antarctica. I better have everything I need."

Hawk looked out the window of the plane. There was snow and ice everywhere. Even though it was winter, the sun shone all day.

"ACME has a pretty good idea that the Guru is living in the center of Antarctica. We think he's living at the top of a mountain. But we don't know exactly where," Mick said.

"It's freezing out there. We could be looking for days!" Hawk said. "RIVAL could find him by then."

"Got any bright ideas, Hawk?" Mick asked.

"I thought the Bosses came up with the bright ideas," Hawk answered.

Mick laughed. He didn't say anything for a moment.

"Why don't you call your friend, Samantha Turner? She works for RIVAL. Maybe she can tell you something," Mick said.

"Sam just works for them, but she's not like them," Hawk said.

"Call her anyway, Hawk," Mick said.

Hawk flipped open his cell phone and dialed.

"Sam here," a voice answered. Her voice was not very clear.

"Uh, what's up Sam? It's Hawk," said Hawk.

"Hawk, this a bad time. Can I call you back?" Sam asked.

"Something wrong, Sam?" Hawk asked.

"I'm very busy, Hawk. Gotta go."

Hawk turned to Mick.

"Sorry, Mick. It seemed like she was in a hurry," Hawk said.

"That's OK," said Mick. "I think I got it."

"Huh?" Hawk said.

"I got a trace on your cell phone call to Sam," Mick said. "It came from a few miles away. It seems that Sam is here with RIVAL."

"Maybe ACME should make you one of

the Bosses," Hawk said.

Mick smiled. "The signal probably came from the base of that tall mountain," he said. "Now all we have to do is land on this ice."

CHAPTER 4

Climbing

Mick soon spotted a large blue ice field along the side of the mountain. He landed the C-130 like a pro.

"RIVAL should be close by," Mick said. "We can't be sure how many of them are here."

"We know RIVAL is here, but where is the Guru?" Hawk asked.

"We have to trust ACME's sources. Let's head up to the top of the mountain," Mick said.

13

"That's got to be few thousand feet up!" Hawk said.

"At least," Mick said.

Mick and Hawk put on their gear. The mountain was too steep to climb alone. A rope connected Hawk and Mick. When one man climbed the other held the safety line. The man above put a screw in the mountain. He then put the rope line through the screw. Then the other man climbed. They did this for hours. They rested a few times, but it was hard for Hawk to take a nap in constant daylight.

Suddenly it started to snow hard. Hawk looked up at Mick. He could barely see him.

"I'm sweating in the cold," Hawk yelled up to Mick.

Mick looked down the mountain. He could barely see the plane. "I hate to do this, Hawk," Mick said, as he continued to look down.

Hawk wondered what Mick was thinking.

"I think you're going to have to go the rest of the way alone," Mick yelled down to Hawk.

"What do you mean?" Hawk asked.

"It's starting to snow hard. We can't let snow form around the plane on the ice field. I better go down and clear it, or we may not be able to leave for days," Mick said.

"But there's still about 500 feet to the top," Hawk said.

"I think you're going to have to go the rest of the way alone," Mick yelled down.

"It doesn't seem quite as steep as before," Mick said. "But don't take any chances, Hawk. If you get stuck, signal me. Don't use your phone. RIVAL may be able to pick up your signal."

"Whatever you say, Mick," Hawk said.

CHAPTER 5

The Guru

Mick headed down the mountain. Hawk climbed up about 50 feet to where Mick had stood before he started back down. There was a small ledge where Hawk could barely stand. He looked around.

Through the falling snow he thought he saw a crack in the side of the mountain. He walked along the ledge towards it. The crack was an opening about four feet tall and three feet wide. He looked inside. It looked like a cave.

Hawk decided to go inside to see if he could rest awhile.

Just then his cell phone rang.

"Mick, I think I found something. It looks like an entrance into the mountain. I'm going in to check it out."

"O.K." The connection was very bad. "Where are you?"

"Not far from where you were. Mick? Mick? We got a bad signal."

Suddenly Hawk's phone was knocked from his hand. Hawk turned around. He saw a tall man grab his phone and switch it off.

"RIVAL!" Hawk shouted. He started for the man.

"No, I'm the Guru," the man said. "And I hate to disagree with you, but I think your signal was good enough."

"What do you mean?" Hawk asked. He wasn't at all sure this was the Guru.

"Are you sure that was Mick on the line?" asked the man.

"Why?"

"Because it is not like Mick to be that careless," the man said. "RIVAL could have gotten a fix on my location."

"Damn! You're right! Mick told me not to use the cell phone. How could I have been that... Wait a minute. How do you know Mick?"

The man laughed. "Didn't he tell you?

We're good friends."

Hawk was really confused. "How do I know this isn't another RIVAL trick?" Hawk asked.

"Come," the man said. "I'll tell you as much as I can. Follow me." He walked into the cave.

Hawk didn't move.

"Come on, Hawk. You can trust the Guru."

CHAPTER 6

Friends and Rivals

Hawk and the Guru walked in silence for a few minutes. They went through a tunnel that led into the Guru's home at the top of the mountain. At last, they came into a room about 50 feet wide and 30 feet tall. The room was protected from the harsh weather outside.

"So, you're Hawk Davidson," the Guru finally said.

"How did you know that?" Hawk said.

"Word gets around. You fit the profile,"

the Guru said. "You're up-and-coming. You're a rising star, just like me and Mick and our old friend from RIVAL. But that was years ago."

"You know the owner of RIVAL?" Hawk asked.

"Sure, we were all very good athletes, pioneers in extreme sports. We each had our special talents. We competed together and against each other. But we also respected each other. We paved the way for guys like you," the Guru said.

"And then what happened?" Hawk asked.

"What do you mean?" asked the Guru.

"You all seemed to take different paths.

One started RIVAL, another went to work for ACME, and you…"

"… ended up here? There's a little more to it than that," the Guru said. "For instance, do you know how I got the name 'Guru'?"

"No. In fact, I don't know why, but Mick didn't tell me he knew you," Hawk said.

"Good. Mick's a good man. He keeps his word. Anyway, like I said, we all had our special talents. Skiing and snowboarding were mine. No one could tackle a mountain like me. In fact, I was so good at 'reading' mountains that he gave me the name of Guru."

"So Mick named you the Guru."

"No, our friend at RIVAL did that," said

the Guru.

"And what's his name?" asked Hawk.

"The owner of RIVAL? Mick hasn't told you that either?" the Guru asked.

"No," said Hawk.

"There's a good reason, Hawk. We were all friends at one time. We made a promise to each other..."

Just then they heard some voices in the tunnel.

"That must be RIVAL," the Guru said. "Come on, Hawk. We have to get going."

The Guru led Hawk through another tunnel that went up a few hundred feet. They ended up in another room.

"Where are we going? Are you going to leave with me?" Hawk asked.

"I'm not worried about RIVAL. They don't care about me. Only this." The Guru pointed to a snowboard hanging on the wall of the cave. Hawk stared at it for a while. It didn't look like any snowboard he had ever seen.

"I've never seen anything like it," Hawk said. "What's it called?"

"Um, I call it the Mega-board," the Guru said. "Take it, Hawk, quickly. We don't have much time."

"You're just giving this to ACME!? They're probably going to make thousands of copies. Don't you want to sign a contract? You could make lots of money."

"I'm not giving it to ACME. I'm giving it to Mick. He will know what to do with it."

"I've been thinking about Mick. Could it be that he might be..."

The Guru laughed. "Don't think too much, Hawk. It could drive you nuts. Just keep this in mind. Life is full of choices. We all face things that tempt us – from corporations, from our own inner-self. It's up to you to choose the right path. Life is more than just black and white, but shades of Grey. Understand?"

"Maybe."

"Good, now this way," the Guru said. He

turned and went into another tunnel.

Hawk took the Mega-board and followed the Guru. "I can't wait to ride this," Hawk said.

"I'm glad you said that, Hawk."

CHAPTER 7

Game Over

Hawk and the Guru could hear a few RIVAL climbers going through the tunnel below. The Guru led Hawk through another small passage that led to an exit. They were now at the very top of the mountain. The snow had stopped, but there was a strong cold wind. The sun shone brightly. Hawk looked down, but he could not see the bottom of the mountain. The cliffs at the top of the mountain blocked the view.

"Get ready, Hawk" the Guru said. "They

29

will soon find us."

"There's no way I'm going down this," Hawk said. "I've never even seen this mountain. I don't know the terrain."

"See that rope over there?" the Guru said. "I'm going to lower you down over the cliff. Then you can snowboard the rest of the way."

Hawk zipped up his jacket and attached the Mega-board to his boots. He then hooked himself to the rope.

"Good luck, Hawk. I know you can do it. Remember, extreme sports are about what's inside yourself – not the gear."

The Guru began to lower Hawk down over the cliff. Hawk could now see the rest of the mountain. He was next to a nearly vertical face.

"How much rope is there?" Hawk shouted up. "I going to need at least a couple of hundred feet to get to a place where I can snowboard down. And, by the way, how do you do this when you're alone?"

"I never use the rope, Hawk. I just jump. Remember, I'm the Guru," the Guru said.

Just then five RIVAL climbers appeared. Sam was with them. She peered over the cliff.

"Hi, Hawk," Sam said. "RIVAL figured you had traced my call, so they did the same to you."

"I see you brought some friends with you," Hawk said. "Sorry to disappoint you, but you're not getting this snowboard."

"The game's over Hawk. We're pulling you back," one of the RIVAL climbers said.

Then Hawk felt a tug on his rope. He was being pulled back up! He had to think quickly. He looked down the mountain and tried to look for a way down.

"Maybe no one could 'read' a mountain like the Guru," thought Hawk, "but I'm going to have to try. After all, the Guru said I'm a rising star."

Then Hawk looked at the Mega-board attached to his boots. "Let's hope this board is worth all the hype," Hawk said.

CHAPTER 8

Tidal Wave

Hawk released himself from his harness.

He fell 10 feet, 20 feet, 30 feet, 50 feet, 100 feet...

But this was no dream! He hit the side of the mountain and bounced off with his snow-board. He fell another 30 feet and then hit again with his snowboard. He tumbled in the air and hit the side of the mountain again. Then he finally gained his balance. The Mega-board, and Hawk, both appeared to be in one piece.

33

The mountain was still really steep. Hawk was struggling to get the hang of the Mega-board. It was unlike anything he had ridden. He looked down the mountain. Hawk guessed he was a few thousand feet from Mick and the plane in the ice field. He tried to find the best way down.

Then Hawk saw three other snowboarders appear next to him. They were waiting for him. They had RIVAL logos on their parkas. Hawk tried to look for another way down, but he could not see one. He dove down into a small crevice. He then turned sharply to avoid some large rocks. Hawk caught some air off a small cliff and did a 720.

No matter what Hawk did, he couldn't

shake the RIVAL snowboarders. Hawk sailed off another edge and flipped over upside down and landed backwards. He was now looking right at the three RIVAL boarders right behind him. They were all wearing goggles and helmets.

"Ready to give up, Hawk?" one of them asked.

Hawk then flipped back around and got into a crouch. He was now going around 60 miles an hour. The Mega-board was performing well, but these snowboarders were good. He might be able to escape one or two, but not all three. One mistake, and it would all be over. It was just a matter of time.

Suddenly, it seemed like the entire

mountain started to shake. Hawk looked around. Snow was starting to break up all around him.

"Avalanche!" yelled one of the RIVAL snowboarders.

Hawk stopped doing tricks and rode down into a small open valley. The RIVAL boarders followed. A huge tidal wave of snow was now roaring down the mountain behind them. Hawk was now going around 80 miles an hour.

The Mega-board was holding up well. Hawk knew he would need more speed. He looked back to see a wall of snow that was almost on top of them. The sound was deafening. Hawk

He was now looking right at the three RIVAL boarders right behind him.

heard one of the snowboarders scream as he lost control. The avalanche then caught the other two RIVAL boarders.

Hawk got further into his crouch. His speed increased to nearly 100 miles per hour. He was feeling a lot of 'chatter' from the Mega-board. Now the huge wave of snow was right behind him. Bits of snow were pelting Hawk's back. He prepared for the worst.

CHAPTER 9

Mission Complete?

Hawk saw a cliff up ahead. He had no choice but to jump. He tried to catch as much air as he possible could. Tons of snow roared right under Hawk and the Mega-board. He then came down right behind it. The avalanche began to slow down and finally stopped a few hundred feet later. Hawk stopped to catch his breath. He couldn't believe he had survived.

Hawk called Sam on his cell phone.

"Sam here," Sam said.

"There's been an avalanche," Hawk said. "Look for three snowboarders."

"Hawk, is that you?" Sam said.

Hawk quickly flipped off the phone.

He took a look around. He could see Mick's plane in the distance. He snowboarded over to it. The runway and the C-130 Hercules plane appeared to be in good shape. Hawk did not see Mick. He took off the snowboard and opened the door of the plane.

"Mick!" Hawk yelled. Mick was sitting in the pilot's seat. "I got the snowboard. The Guru said you would know what to do with it." Mick looked at the board, smiled, and then looked at Hawk.

Mick still didn't say a word. He just looked at Hawk, and then toward the back of the plane. Hawk turned and saw four more RIVAL members sitting in the back of the plane.

"Give them the board, Hawk. There's too many of them. They won this round." Mick said. He still didn't move. Hawk now saw that Mick's hands were tied to the pilot's seat.

"He's right, Hawk. Give us the snowboard and we'll be on our way. Then you can untie Mick and get out of here," one of the RIVAL boarders said.

There was nothing Hawk could do. He handed over the Mega-board. The RIVAL members got out of the plane and left.

"Give them the board, Hawk. There's too many of them. They won this round."

Hawk then untied Mick. "Come on, Mick. We can still catch them!"

"Let them go," Mick said.

"But what about the Mega-board? The Guru, I mean your friend, said you would know what to do with it."

Mick laughed, and started the plane. "He was right. That 'Mega-board' is over 20 years old. It was advanced for its time, but it's not worth much of anything now. When RIVAL finds out about it, they won't be too happy."

"But I've never seen anything like it," Hawk said.

"That's because that board is older than you are, Hawk. And as for how it performed, I'm afraid that was all in your head. You were the one

who got down that mountain," Mick said. "In the

end, Hawk, it's about the person – not the gear."

"Funny, that's what the Guru said, too,"

Hawk said.